# Lily's Pesky Plant

# Lily's Pesky Plant

WRITTEN BY
KIRSTEN LARSEN

ILLUSTRATED BY
JUDITH HOLMES CLARKE
& THE DISNEY STORYBOOK ARTISTS

HarperCollins *Children's Books*

First published in the USA by Disney Press,
114 Fifth Avenue, New York, New York, 10011-5690.

First published in Great Britain in 2006
by HarperCollins Children's Books.
HarperCollins Children's Books is a division of
HarperCollins Publishers,
77 - 85 Fulham Palace Road, Hammersmith, London, W6 8JB.

The HarperCollins Children's Books website is
www.harpercollinschildrensbooks.co.uk

978-0-00-720933-0

0-00-720933-9

4

Printed and bound in Great Britain by Clays Ltd,
St Ives plc.

Visit disneyfairies.com

# All About Fairies

IF YOU HEAD toward the second star on your right and fly straight on till morning, you'll come to Never Land, a magical island where mermaids play and children never grow up.

When you arrive, you might hear something like the tinkling of little bells. Follow that sound and you'll find Pixie Hollow, the secret heart of Never Land.

A great old maple tree grows in Pixie Hollow, and in it live hundreds of fairies and sparrow men. Some of them can do water magic, others can fly like the wind, and still others can speak to animals. You see, Pixie Hollow is the Never fairies' kingdom, and each fairy who lives there has a special, extraordinary talent.

Not far from the Home Tree, nestled in the branches of a hawthorn, is Mother Dove, the most magical creature of all. She sits on her egg, watching over the fairies, who in turn watch over her. For as long as Mother Dove's egg stays well and whole, no one in Never Land will ever grow old.

Once, Mother Dove's egg *was* broken. But we are not telling the story of the egg here. Now it is time for Lily's tale...

Lily's
Pesky
Plant

# 1

EARLY ONE MORNING, Lily woke to the sound of birds chirping in the topmost branches of the Home Tree, the ancient maple where Never Land's fairies live. Opening her eyes, she saw the walls of her room stretch ever so slightly as the great tree reached its branches toward the early morning sun. Lily pushed back her fern frond quilt and yawned, stretching her arms up into the air.

Lily climbed out of bed and opened the doors of her wardrobe, which was made from a dried gourd. She chose a thistledown shirt and knickers woven from dandelion fluff. Unlike some fairies, Lily didn't like spider-silk gowns and shoes with heels as thin as pine needles. She liked simple, sturdy clothes.

In the tearoom, Lily had her usual breakfast, a cup of lemongrass tea and a slice of poppy seed cake. Some of the other garden-talent fairies at Lily's table sat for a while at breakfast. They refilled their pots of tea and spread heaps of black cherry jam on their bread. But not Lily. The moment her plate and cup were empty, she pushed them aside and flew off to her garden.

Lily's garden was just two frog's leaps beyond the Home Tree, right in the heart of Pixie Hollow. All the fairies agreed that it was one of the nicest places in the entire fairy kingdom. On one side of her garden was a hedge of raspberry bushes. On the other side, a wild rosebush sweetly scented the air. Everywhere bright red and orange poppies sprang from the ground. Clusters of Queen Anne's lace and lilac made pleasant groves where a fairy could sit and think. And throughout the garden, sweet clover sprouted in fairy-sized beds. They were perfect for taking naps in.

The garden was a favourite spot of many fairies, who were always dropping by. Harvest-talent fairies picked raspberries from the bushes. Healing-talent fairies collected herbs for their potions. Other fairies simply liked to walk among the beautiful flowers.

Lily welcomed them all. Next to working in her garden, Lily's favourite thing was watching fairies enjoy the beautiful plants she grew. The fairies also enjoyed Lily's company. With her friendly, direct smile and her sparkling dark eyes, she was as fresh and lovely as the flowers she grew.

As soon as Lily got to her garden, she called out, "Bumble!" At once, a large bee zipped out of the flowers and flew up to her. Bumble was yellow, round, and fuzzy all over. He wasn't Lily's pet, exactly. He had just showed up one day and never left. The two had become good friends.

Bumble always followed Lily as she took care of her plants. She watered them. She checked their leaves for spots. That morning Lily saw that some of the daffodils had been toppled by a breeze. She tied the stems to stakes to help them stand sturdy and strong again.

When she was done making the rounds in her garden, Lily lay down on a patch of soft moss to watch the grass grow. To you this might sound boring, but for her it was every bit as exciting as watching butterfly races (a favourite fairy pastime). Lily was certain that the blades of grass grew faster when they knew she was watching.

Unluckily for Lily, she was the only fairy in all of Pixie Hollow to have this hobby. When others saw her lying in the grass, they usually thought she was doing nothing at all. Often, they would start talking to her. This frustrated Lily, for it broke her concentration.

And that was exactly what happened that morning. Bumble was buzzing around the buttercups in the corner of her garden, and Lily was lying nearby, watching a (very slow) race between two blades of grass. One blade was winning, and Lily was urging the other one to catch up, when a voice broke through her thoughts.

"I say, what a funny thing!" The voice

was loud and a bit shrill.

Lily didn't move, except to lower her eyelids. She hoped whoever it was would think she was sleeping and go away.

"I said, what a funny thing!" the voice cried, even more shrilly.

Lily sighed and opened her eyes. A tall fairy was standing over her. She had curly hair the colour of a wax bean and a long, narrow nose that was red at the tip.

"Hello, Iris," said Lily, sitting up. "What's so funny?"

"Why, just look at your buttercups."

Lily looked. She didn't see anything funny about them.

"They're the biggest I've ever seen!" Iris exclaimed. "You ought to call them butter-*bowls* instead." She chuckled at her own joke.

Lily smiled politely. "They do seem

happy," she replied. Lily didn't care how big or small a plant was, as long as it was happy. That was the reason the plants in her garden grew so well – she made sure they were all content.

"Of course, they're nothing like the buttercups I used to grow," Iris went on. "They were as big as soup pots and yellow as the sun. I'll tell you a secret I learned from a Tiffen: you have to give them *real butter*."

Lily raised her eyebrows in surprise. The Tiffens were big-eared creatures who grew bananas. Their farms weren't far from Pixie Hollow. Lily had never heard of a Tiffen who grew buttercups.

*Then again*, she thought, *what do I know about Tiffens?* Lily didn't spend very much time outside her garden.

Iris gave her a smug little nod. Like

Lily, Iris was a garden-talent fairy. She had once had her own garden, but it was so long ago no one could remember what it had been like.

Then Iris had begun writing her plant book. Now, she claimed, she was much too busy to do any real gardening. Instead, she went around poking her nose into other fairies' gardens. She said she was collecting information for her book. But she usually did more talking than listening.

Lily couldn't imagine what it would be like to be a garden fairy without a garden. She thought it must be awful.

Iris plopped down on a spotted red toadstool and flipped open the birch bark cover of her book. She turned its pages, which were made from leaves. Iris carried the book with her everywhere she went.

"Anyway, Lily," Iris said, "I've come because I'm worried about your snapdragons. Now, don't get me wrong. They seem perfectly healthy and strong. But when I went to take a peek at their petals the other day, one snapped at me!"

"They're *snap*dragons, Iris," Lily pointed out patiently. "It's their nature to be cranky."

"Well, I *know* a thing or two about snapdragons, Lily," Iris said. "And you can't just let them act wild. You've got to *train* them." Iris continued to flip through the pages of her book. "I found a perfectly brilliant way to keep them from snapping." She tapped the page she'd opened to. "Here, I'll read it to you. 'A Cure for Snappish Snapdragons, by Iris. If your snapdragons have bad manners, you must pinch their leaves whenever they snap at you... '"

As Iris read on, Lily's toes began to wiggle impatiently. Suddenly, she blurted out, "Actually, Iris, I was just about to leave."

It wasn't true, and Lily wasn't quite sure why she'd said it. She knew Iris only meant to be helpful. But maybe she was annoyed with Iris for interrupting her peaceful morning. Or maybe it was just that Lily *liked* her snapdragons to be snappish. Whatever the reason, on this particular day, Lily just didn't feel like listening to Iris.

"Where are you going? I could come with you and tell you more on the way," Iris offered.

"Oh, but... I'm going fern spotting. Possum ferns, that is," Lily said quickly. Any fairy knew it was impossible to look for possum ferns and talk at the same time. The ferns were shy and would wilt completely if they heard a noise.

"Oh. Okay, then. Another time." Iris blew her nose into a leafkerchief. She looked disappointed, and Lily felt a little pang. She wished she hadn't lied about going to the forest. But it was too late to take it back now.

"Yes, another time. See you, Iris," Lily said. She rose into the air and flew off into the forest.

When she was just out of sight from the garden, Lily landed near the roots of an old oak tree.

"I'll just go for a short walk," she told herself as she set out along a narrow path through the bushes. "Then I'll go back." She figured Iris would have moved to someone else's garden by then.

Most fairies never went to the forest alone because of snakes, owls, and hawks. And fairies almost never walked unless their wings were too wet to fly. But Lily was brave, and what was more, she liked walking. She felt closer to the plants when her feet were on the ground.

Lily walked along the forest floor. She kept an eye out for snakes. High above, the wind rustled the leaves of the trees. Lily took off her shoes. She liked the feeling of the damp soil between her toes.

Just then, she spotted something curled against the base of a rock. It was a silvery green plant with tightly coiled, velvety leaves. Lily smiled.

"A possum fern!" she whispered. She had spotted one after all! Holding her breath, Lily silently crept toward the rare plant to get a closer look.

Suddenly, something crashed through the leaves over her head. Lily gasped and flew for cover between the roots of a nearby tree. Had a hawk just swooped at her? Trembling, she peered out from behind the root and scanned the forest.

But there was no sign of a hawk. The forest was still and quiet. Lily looked over at the possum fern and saw that its leaves had uncoiled and turned brown. It had heard the noise and was playing dead.

Then Lily saw something that made her gasp again. In the spot where she had just been standing lay a strange seed.

## 2

AT LEAST, LILY thought it was a seed. It was hard to say for sure. She had never seen anything quite like it before.

It was as big as a chestnut and a pearly white colour, like the inside of an oyster shell. The ends tapered into points. A few fibers stuck out like hairs from the tips.

As soon as her heart stopped racing, Lily flew over and landed next to the strange object. She picked up a twig and poked it. Nothing happened.

Lily felt braver. She touched it with her fingertips. The surface felt cool and smooth, like a sea-polished rock.

Now Lily was sure it was a seed. Her gardening instincts told her there was life inside it – the sleeping life of a plant waiting to grow.

"But where did it come from?" Lily asked aloud.

Just then, she heard a loud chittering sound above her. She looked up. A squirrel was chattering at her from a branch overhead.

Lily laughed. Now she knew where the seed had come from. The squirrel probably wasn't used to seeing fairies walking on the ground. It had dropped the seed in surprise.

"Don't worry," she called to the squirrel. "I'm leaving soon!" The squirrel chattered at her again, then darted away along a tree branch.

Lily looked back down at the seed. *What is it?* she wondered. For once, she wished she were an animal-talent fairy. Then she could talk to the squirrel and ask him where the mysterious seed had come from.

"What kind of plant are you?" Lily whispered to the seed. As she said the words, something occurred to her, and her eyes widened. "That's it!" she exclaimed. "I'll plant it! After all, the only way to find out what a seed will become is to watch it grow."

Lily reached down to pick it up. To her surprise, it was heavy. She sprinkled a pinch of fairy dust over the seed. It grew lighter in her arms.

Clutching her treasure against her chest, Lily rose into the air and flew in the direction of her garden.

Back at her garden, Lily found Iris still sitting on the toadstool, right where she had left her.

"Oh, Lily, you're back already," said Iris. "Did you get to see some possum ferns? The last time I went possum fern spotting, I saw exactly three dozen of them. Although for some reason, they all were playing dead... ”

"I found something even better," Lily told Iris. She no longer felt annoyed with her. She was much too excited about her find. Gently Lily placed the big seed on the ground.

Iris was so surprised, she sneezed three times in a row. "What an amazing seed!" she cried, after she'd blown her nose. "Whatever is it?"

"You don't know?" Lily asked. "I was hoping you would. I found it in the forest just now. I've never seen one before."

Bumble heard Lily's voice and flew over to greet her. Lily patted his fuzzy side.

"What do you think of my new seed, Bumble?" she asked.

The bee landed on the seed, paused for a moment, then flew off in the direction of the roses. Bumble was more interested in flowers than seeds.

Iris squinted closely at the seed. Then she pulled out her writing splinter and made a note in her book. She began to draw a picture of the seed next to it.

"Hi, Lily. Hi, Iris. What is that? It's so lovely!" said a friendly voice. Rani, a pretty water-talent fairy with long, blonde hair, walked over to them.

"Hi, Rani," said Lily. "It's some kind of seed. We're not sure what. I found it today in the – "

" – beach cove?" Rani asked. She had a habit of finishing others' sentences.

"No, the forest," said Lily.

"Oh. It's just that it just reminds me of a shell," Rani said fondly. She squatted down to admire the seed.

"I'll bet that's it," Iris said. She tapped her writing splinter thoughtfully against her cheek. "I'll bet it's a seaweed seed." She made another note in her book.

Lily shrugged. She had no idea what a seaweed seed looked like, or whether there was such a thing. Fairies never went underwater. Their wings would soak up too much water and drag them down.

But Rani shook her head. "No, I don't think so," she said. "I've never seen anything like it before."

Iris frowned. Lily knew Iris didn't like to be wrong. But she couldn't argue with Rani. The water-talent fairy had visited the mermaids in order to help save Never Land, and she had even cut off her wings to do it. She was the only fairy in Never Land who had ever been underwater. On the subject of

19

seaweed seeds, she certainly knew more than anyone in Pixie Hollow.

Scowling, Iris crossed out what she had just written.

"Well," said Lily, "there's only one way to find out what it is." She picked up a shovel and drove the tip into the ground.

Iris looked up from her book. "You're going to plant it? Just like that?" she asked. She sounded alarmed. "But you don't know how much sunlight it needs. Or how much water. And what if it doesn't get along with the other flowers? And... and... "

Lily smiled. Iris certainly knew a lot about plants. *But knowing about plants isn't all there is to gardening,* Lily thought. *Some-times you just have to trust your instincts.*

"I'm sure everything will be fine," she said.

# 3

"WHAT IS THAT sound?" Lily exclaimed.

It was a few days after she had planted the seed. Lily had been wrapping spider silk around some violets that had caught a chill when she was interrupted by a terrible racket. It sounded like big metal teeth chomping together.

*Chomp! Chomp! Chomp!*

Lily cupped her hands over her ears. The sound was coming from the other side of her garden. She hurried toward it.

Suddenly, Lily stopped short in surprise. There was Iris, sitting atop a strange contraption.

It had a seat and pedals. At the front of the machine was a set of huge metal jaws. As Lily watched, Iris dumped a bucket of kitchen garbage into the jaws. Then she put her feet on the pedals. As her legs moved, the metal jaws chewed up the garbage.

*Chomp! Chomp! Chomp!*

"Just making a little food for our seed!" Iris shouted over the noise. She stopped pedaling and held up a bucket for Lily to see. It was full of mulched vegetable scraps.

"It's chock-full of nutrients for a growing plant." Iris beamed proudly.

Bumble flew around Lily in dizzy circles. He hated loud noises.

"Well, that's... very thoughtful, Iris," said Lily. She eyed the machine uncertainly.

"Only the best for our little plant," Iris said. She went back to pedaling. Lily winced and put her hands over her ears.

Ever since Lily had planted the mysterious seed, Iris had come to her

22

garden every day to check on it. And each time, she had some new idea for how to make the plant grow faster.

One day Iris had turned up with a daisy umbrella, insisting that the seed would grow best in the shade. The next day she fretted that it wasn't getting the sunlight it needed. In the afternoons, Iris would sit on the spotted toadstool, talking about the seed and writing in her book.

"It's not every day that someone finds a new plant," Iris told Lily. "I'm writing everything down. You know, for future garden fairies."

Lily just smiled. Iris was the only garden fairy she knew who liked to read about gardening. The other fairies just *gardened*. Still, she couldn't blame Iris for being excited. Lily was just as curious to see what kind of plant would grow.

Iris finally finished mulching the garbage. She picked up the bucket of plant food and set off in the direction of the seed. Lily went back to tending her violets.

Suddenly, Iris shrieked.

Lily dropped the spider silk and raced back to the toadstool. Maybe Iris had hurt herself! But the red-nosed fairy was grinning from ear to ear. "Look, Lily!" she said breathlessly. "It sprouted!"

Lily looked where Iris was pointing. Sure enough, a small seedling was growing where they'd planted the mysterious seed.

Lily clapped her hands together. "Oh, it's beautiful," she whispered.

In fact, the seedling wasn't beautiful at all. Its leaves were a sickly yellow colour. Its stem was covered with little spots, as if it had a bad case of chicken pox. But that was the thing about Lily. She thought every plant was beautiful.

Iris was thrilled. "Vidia!" she called out to a fairy passing by. "Come look at our new little plant!"

Vidia flew over to them. She looked at the seedling and made a face. "Darlings, I've never seen anything so ugly in my life," she declared.

Iris's face fell. Lily frowned. *Trust Vidia to say something mean*, she thought. The dark-haired, fast-flying fairy was as spiteful as they came.

"It reminds me of a sick caterpillar I saw once," Vidia went on. "If I were you, I'd put it out of its misery now. Iris, dear, why don't you run along and get a shovel to dig it up?"

Iris's glow flared with anger. She scowled at Vidia.

Lily ignored Vidia. "Iris, let's give it water," she said. "It looks like it could use some."

Iris gave Vidia one last angry glance. Then she picked up a bucket and hurried off to the stream.

"Lily, dear, how can you stand having her around all the time?" Vidia said. She glanced at Iris's back. "A garden fairy without a garden." She shook her head. "*Tsk, tsk.* How sad." But Vidia didn't sound sad. She sounded amused.

"She's better company than *some* fairies," Lily replied.

Vidia gave her a sugary smile. "I can take a hint, sweetie," she said. "Have fun with your little sprout. But you should watch out for those spots. They look contagious."

Rising into the air, Vidia put on a burst of speed and disappeared.

For the next several days, Lily and Iris carefully tended the plant. They watered it every morning. They talked to it every afternoon. The seedling seemed to enjoy the attention. It grew amazingly fast. Soon it towered over the fairies' heads.

It grew uglier, too. The small spots grew into big warts. Sticky sap dripped from its bark. It sprouted thin, droopy branches. Sometimes Lily thought Vidia was right. It *did* look a bit like a sick caterpillar – a great big sick caterpillar with droopy legs.

Lily didn't care. She could tell that the plant was happy, so she was happy, too.

The other fairies weren't quite so open-minded. "Lily, come quick!" Tinker Bell burst into the tearoom one morning. "I just flew past your garden. A monster is attacking your buttercups!"

Lily dropped her teacup and the two fairies raced out of the Home Tree.

Outside Lily's garden, they paused behind the rosebush. With silent looks they agreed they would take the beast by surprise. Tinker Bell drew her dagger. The two fairies crept forward.

"There it is!" Tink whispered, pointing.

Lily began to laugh. She laughed until tears rolled down her cheeks.

Tink stared at her in surprise.

At last Lily flew over and landed beside the "monster." "Tink," she said between chuckles, "meet my newest plant."

"That's a *plant?*" Tink said. She blushed and lowered her dagger. Taking a few steps forward, she peered up at its ugly branches. "What kind is it?"

"I don't know. I found the seed in the forest and planted it," Lily explained.

"Well, it's very interesting," replied Tink. "But I'd hate to bump into it on a dark night."

Even the other garden fairies were doubtful. "I've never seen anything like it," said Rosetta. "Are you sure you want such an ugly plant in your garden?"

"I'm sure," said Lily.

The other fairies looked around at the beautiful flowers and shook their heads. But they didn't say anything more. If nothing else, they thought, the mysterious plant kept Iris away from *their* gardens.

# 4

ONE MORNING, LILY noticed a strange odour in her garden. It smelled like rotten tomatoes, and a little bit like sour milk.

*How odd*, Lily thought. She began to walk through her garden, looking for the source of the stink.

Soon she came to the red spotted toadstool. It was empty. Iris hadn't yet arrived.

Lily covered her nose with her hands. The smell was even stronger here.

Bumble, who had followed her, began to flit around nervously. Suddenly, he darted away.

"I wonder what's gotten into him?" Lily said to herself.

She turned and saw something that made her forget all about Bumble. The mysterious plant had grown flowers. And what strange flowers! They practically exploded from its branches. The centers of the giant flowers were pale and sticky-looking. Spiky white petals stuck out from the edges, like crazy uncombed hair.

The flowers were not pretty. But in their own way they were interesting, Lily thought.

Curious, she rose into the air until she was face to face with one of the flowers. She leaned forward, closed her eyes, and...

*Ugh!* Lily's eyes flew open. Her wings froze in midflutter. She dropped out of the air and landed on the ground with a painful thud.

The horrible rotten-tomato smell was coming from the flowers.

*Bzzzzzzzzzzzzz!*

Bumble zipped over to Lily to see if she

was okay. A moment later he darted away again. He couldn't stand the flowers' smell.

"Lily, are you all right?" asked a muffled voice.

Lily looked up and saw Iris hurrying over to her. She was holding a leafkerchief over her nose and mouth. "I saw you fall," she told Lily.

"I'm all right," Lily replied. She rubbed a bruised spot on her knee. "Just surprised. I really wasn't expecting it to... *stink* so much!"

Iris held out a clean leafkerchief. Lily took it gratefully. Covering their noses, the two fairies stared up at the big, smelly flowers. Iris looked worried.

"You've gone and spoiled it," Iris complained. "That's what happens when you baby plants. They develop obnoxious personalities."

Behind her leafkerchief, Lily smiled. Iris had babied the plant even more than Lily had.

But Lily didn't think that was the problem. In fact, she didn't think there was any problem. She had a feeling that the plant was doing exactly what it was supposed to do.

Before she could say so, other voices interrupted.

"What *is* that smell?"

"It's as if all the food in the kitchen went bad!"

"It's coming from over there!"

A little group of fairies and sparrow men came flying toward them from the Home Tree. They were all wearing clothespegs on their noses. They came to a sudden stop when they saw the giant flowers.

"Goodness!"

"How ugly!"

"*That's* what smells so bad."

"Lily, what in the name of Never Land is wrong with that plant?" asked Dulcie, a baking-talent fairy. Her voice sounded funny because of the clothespeg pinching her nose.

"Nothing," replied Lily. "I don't think there's anything wrong with it."

"Well, can you do something about that smell? It's blowing in the windows of the tearoom," said a serving-talent sparrow man. "Queen Ree sent us to find out where it was coming from." Ree was the fairies' nickname for Queen Clarion.

Lily looked around. Her eyes fell on a patch of lavender.

"I have an idea," she said. Hurrying

over to her lavender, she picked a few pieces. She tucked a bit inside her leaf-kerchief and tied it around her nose and mouth like a mask. The lavender's sweetness covered up the bad smell.

She handed the rest of the lavender to the other fairies. They pinned the flowers to their noses with the clothespins. Then Lily returned to the lavender bush and began filling her arms with flowers.

"Everyone come pick some," she instructed. "We can take it back to the other fairies in the Home Tree."

Just then, she heard a sound.

BZZZZZZZZZZZZZZZZZZ...

At first Lily thought Bumble had gotten his head stuck in a flower (it happened sometimes) and was buzzing for help. But the sound grew louder.

BZZZZZZZZZZZZZZZZZ...

She looked up. A black cloud seemed to be moving toward them across the sky.

BZZZZZZZZZZZZZZZZZ...

Lily looked closer. It wasn't a cloud at all. It was a huge swarm of wasps!

"Look out!" Lily cried.

The fairies leaped into the lavender for cover as the wasps dove toward them. Nearby, Bumble hid in a patch of clover.

But the wasps weren't after the fairies. Buzzing loudly, they clustered around the flowers on the mysterious plant. They seemed to like the strange, stinky smell.

In the lavender, the fairies waited... and waited and waited. They hoped the wasps would get tired of the flowers and go away.

But the swarm only grew.

Lily's legs began to feel cramped from crouching so long.

"What do we do now?" Dulcie whispered to Lily.

Lily sighed. She had no idea what to do. They couldn't make a dash for the Home Tree because they might get stung. A single sting could be fatal to a fairy – after all, the wasps were nearly as big as their heads. But they couldn't hide in the lavender forever.

Just then, Lily heard a caw. She peeped out of the lavender and saw a large black shape swoop down from the sky. Another dark shape followed right behind it.

Ravens!

And riding on the ravens' backs, right between their wings, were fairies.

# 5

THE RAVENS DOVE at the wasps. They flapped their wings and cawed fiercely. The swarm began to break up. The wasps were afraid of the huge black birds.

Finally, the last wasp was gone. Lily and the other fairies climbed out of the lavender.

The ravens landed next to them. On their backs were Beck and Fawn, two animal-talent fairies.

"A scout saw the swarm go into your garden," Beck explained. "We thought there might be trouble. So we called the ravens."

Beck said something to the ravens that Lily couldn't understand. Then she and Fawn fluttered to the ground. With a great rustle of feathers, the birds stretched their enormous wings and flew away.

"Is anyone hurt?" asked Fawn.

Iris, who had been silent, suddenly burst into tears. "I nearly got stung!" she cried. "A wasp came this close to me!" She held her hands an inch apart.

Some of the fairies from the kitchen frowned. After all, everyone had been in danger. Yet Iris seemed concerned only about herself.

Fawn gently patted Iris's back to calm her down. She was used to taking care of frightened animals. Frightened fairies weren't that different.

"Anyone else?" asked Beck.

The other fairies and sparrow men shook their heads. They were all scared, but no one had been harmed.

"Come on, Iris," Beck said. "Let's go back to the Home Tree. A cup of tea with honey will make you feel better."

"And in the meantime, someone ought to do something about that plant," Fawn added.

"What do you mean 'do something'?" Lily asked.

"Well, chop it down or pull it up. You know, get rid of it," Fawn said.

Lily drew back as if she'd been slapped. Chop down a plant? Just hearing the words made her legs ache. She had never chopped down a plant in her life. She couldn't even pull weeds from her garden – instead, she encouraged them to grow elsewhere.

"The wasps liked those flowers," Fawn explained. "They could come back at any moment."

Lily looked at Iris. She hoped Iris would say something good about the plant. After all, Iris loved it as much as Lily did.

Iris's eyes were wide and her face was pale. But she didn't say anything.

Lily turned back to Beck and Fawn. "The plant is growing in my garden," she said. "I will take responsibility for it." She looked at Dulcie and the other fairies from the kitchen. "Tell the others in the tearoom. You have my word that no one will be endangered here again."

There was a long pause. "All right," Dulcie said at last. "I'll tell the queen you'll take care of the smell."

The little band of fairies headed back to the Home Tree.

As Beck led her away, Iris glanced back at Lily. Lily thought she looked sorry. But she couldn't say for sure.

For the next few days, Lily was very busy. Every morning she picked armloads of lavender to hand out to the fairies of Pixie Hollow. Her leaf kerchief masks were a good way to cover up the smell of the stinky flowers. But it took a lot of lavender to keep everyone happy. Lily's lavender plants were starting to look bare. What would happen when she ran out?

She also worried that the wasps would come back. Every day, she searched the sky for signs of a buzzing black cloud. But the sky remained blue. The only clouds she saw were fluffy and white.

Then one morning, Lily woke with a stuffy nose. Her eyes watered and her throat itched. Her whole head felt as if it were filled with cotton.

"What a terrible time to catch a cold," Lily said as she climbed out of bed. She dressed slowly. She was already thinking of the work that lay ahead of her. She had to hand out more lavender, and she was behind in her gardening.

When she got to the tearoom, Lily noticed something strange. None of the fairies had on a leafkerchief mask. Instead, they were using their leafkerchiefs to blow their noses. Everyone in the Home Tree seemed to be sick.

"Hi, Lily," the other garden fairies said as she sat down at their table. Lily looked around. All the fairies had watery eyes and runny noses. Some had dandelion-fluff scarves wrapped around their throats. Only

Iris looked the same as usual – maybe because she always looked as if she had a cold.

"What an awful cold everyone's got," Lily remarked as she filled her teacup.

"Oh, it's no cold," Rosetta replied stuffily. She dabbed at her nose with a rose petal. "It's that pink dust."

"Pink dust?" asked Lily.

Rosetta nodded. "It's everywhere. The cleaning-talent fairies can't get rid of it. It makes them sneeze so much, they can't get any work done."

A bleary-eyed serving-talent fairy came to the table to serve their tea. All the teacups were covered with a strange, sticky pink dust.

Suddenly, Lily had a bad feeling. "I'll be right back," she said. She hurried off to her garden.

Sure enough, her entire garden looked as if it had been covered in pink snow. When a slight breeze blew, more pink dust floated down from the flowers on the mysterious plant.

It wasn't dust, Lily realised. It was pollen. And everyone in Pixie Hollow was allergic to it!

## 6

By afternoon, pink pollen covered Pixie Hollow. It floated in the fairies' chestnut soup at lunch. It stuck in their hair. It gummed up their wings. And, of course, it made everyone sneeze.

Iris made *tsk-tsk* noises from her spot on the toadstool. "I told you not to plant that seed without knowing anything about it," she said. She sneezed twice and blew her nose, then looked thoughtfully at the plant. "Still," she added, "it *is* a most extraordinary plant."

Lily frowned at her, but Iris didn't notice. She had already gone back to scribbling in her book.

Just then, a fairy bolted into the garden. She screeched to a stop right in front of Lily. It was Vidia. And she looked furious.

"You should have uprooted that... that *thing* when it was a sprout," Vidia snarled. As she spoke, she tried to shake the sticky pollen from her wings. Vidia despised anything that kept her from flying fast. She was so angry, she hadn't even bothered to call Lily dear or darling.

"Here, let me wash your wings, Vidia," Lily said. It was a special kindness to offer to wash another fairy's wings. Lily felt sorry that Vidia was so upset, and it was her way of saying so.

"*I'm* the only fairy who touches my wings," Vidia snapped. She turned and pointed at the tree. "If *you* won't cut it down, I *will*. I'm sure one of the carpenter-talent fairies would be happy to loan me an axe."

And for what might have been the first time in the history of Pixie Hollow, many of the fairies agreed with Vidia. All afternoon, fairies came to Lily to complain about the plant.

"*Ah-choo!* I've had to throw out three acorn puffs," Dulcie told Lily. "Every time I... I... I – *ah-choo!* – sneeze, the puffs collapse! If there's nothing to eat at dinner tonight, you can blame that plant of yours."

Even Terence, a normally cheerful dust-talent sparrow man, was troubled. "That pink stuff has gotten mixed in with the fairy dust," he told Lily. "It's messing up everyone's magic. The music-talent fairies' instruments will only play in the key of B minor. And the laundry fairies haven't been able to do the wash. Their soap went haywire and the washroom is eight inches

48

deep in bubbles! Before you know it," he added grimly, "we won't even be able to fly."

Later, Lily found a quiet patch of clover and sat down alone. All day, not a single fairy had come to smell the roses or walk among the flowers of her garden. They had come only to complain.

Bumble saw Lily's slumped shoulders and sad expression. He flew over to her and gently bumped her arm.

When Lily didn't respond, Bumble flew in crazy loops and zigzags. He was pretending he'd had too much pollen. Usually that made Lily laugh.

But Lily didn't even smile. "Not now, Bumble," she said with a sigh.

Lily saw Iris flying toward her. Lily wished she would go away. She didn't need to hear another "I told you so."

"What a day, huh?" Iris said as she landed in front of Lily.

Lily shrugged.

"Look on the bright side, Lily," Iris said. She sat down beside her in the clover. "Everyone's nose is so stuffed up, no one can *smell* those stinky flowers anymore."

Lily laughed. But a second later her smile faded.

"All the other fairies want me to fix the plant," she told Iris. "But what can I do? Can you stop the clouds from raining? Can you stop the wind from blowing? The plant is just doing what it normally does."

She glanced over at the plant. Despite its ugliness, awful smell, and itchy pollen, there was something special about it.

"The thing is," Lily added, "I think there's more to it than just what we've seen."

Iris nodded. "I feel the same way." A look of alarm crossed her face as another thought occurred to her. "Do you think it could be something bad?" she asked. "After all, it's already caused so much trouble..."

Lily shook her head. "I don't think so. I always know when there's real trouble, because the plants in my garden tell me," she explained. "When they're tense, I know a big storm is coming. If there's a fire anywhere in the forest, my flowers let me know even before I can smell smoke. But since I planted that strange seed in my garden, the other plants seem as happy and healthy as ever."

Iris looked around. It was true. The garden was bursting with colour. Even the leaves of the clover they were sitting in seemed greener and fuller than usual.

"If the plant were really bad, my garden wouldn't look so good." Lily sighed. "But all the other fairies are so angry with me. I don't know what to do. I want the plants in my garden to make other fairies happy, not miserable."

"They make me happy," Iris said quietly. She looked down and plucked at a cloverleaf. Then she said, "I should have stood up for our plant that day when the wasps came. It was wrong that I didn't."

Lily looked at her and knew that she meant it.

"It's okay," she said.

"I like gardening with you," Iris went on. "None of the other garden fairies like to have me in their gardens. I know what they say behind my back, you know. They say I'm incomplete."

Lily swallowed hard. Before fairies became fairies, they were laughs. But sometimes a bit of laugh broke off and the fairy ended up with something missing. A fairy like that was called "incomplete."

Lily had heard other garden fairies say that about Iris. She hadn't realised that Iris had heard it as well. Suddenly, she felt sorry about the times when she'd wished Iris would go away.

"You're not incomplete," Lily told her.

"Maybe I am," Iris said. "I love plants as much as any garden fairy. But growing them doesn't come naturally to me the way it does to you. You know, I fibbed about the buttercups in my garden. They weren't as big as soup pots. In fact, they weren't very big at all."

Lily looked surprised. Iris had always

made a big deal about her garden.

Iris nodded, ashamed. "I could never keep things straight in my head. Which plants need shade, which like more sun. Which plants like to be watered in the morning, and which like water at night. That's why I started to write things down. Then I got carried away. I started to write down everything I'd ever heard about all the plants in Never Land." She shook her head. "But I guess it's not the same as having a garden."

Lily thought about this for a moment. Then she smiled. "You do have a garden," she said.

Iris looked confused.

"Right here." Lily tapped the cover of Iris's plant book. "Your garden is on these pages. I'll bet it has more plants than any garden in Pixie Hollow."

Now Iris smiled. For a while, the two fairies sat quietly with their arms hooked around their knees. They looked up at the strange, ugly plant.

"There *is* something special about that plant," Iris said at last.

"What is that?" asked Lily.

"It made us friends," Iris replied.

That night after dinner, Lily went once more to her garden. She stood for a long time looking at the mysterious plant.

"Where did you come from?" she murmured. "What are you? Why are you causing so many problems?"

A breeze blew. A few more grains of pollen drifted down from the flower. Lily sneezed three times in a row. *Ah-choo! Ah-*

*choo! Ah-choo!*

The wind shifted, and suddenly Lily sensed a change in the garden. The buttercups, the grass, the lavender, even the mysterious plant all seemed alert. It was as if they were waiting for something.

A raindrop fell from the sky. It landed on Lily's head, soaking her hair. More raindrops splashed on the ground around her.

Rain! Around Lily, the plants began to perk up. This was what they had been waiting for.

The rain came down harder. Lily stretched out her arms and let herself get drenched. The rain washed the pink pollen out of her hair and off her skin.

By the time Lily left the garden, her wings were too wet to fly. She had to walk all the way back to the Home Tree. But she didn't mind.

That night, she stayed up late. She watched the rain from the window of her room. For the first time in days, Lily felt happy. The rain was scrubbing Pixie Hollow clean, washing all the pollen away.

# 7

LILY STARTED AWAKE. Was it morning? No, her room was still dark. Glancing out her window, she could see that the sky was starting to turn grey. It was just before dawn.

*Why did I wake up?* Lily wondered.

*THUMP!* Something banged against her window.

Startled, Lily climbed out of bed. She crept over to her window and cautiously peered out.

*THUMP!* A yellow and black shape threw itself against the window.

Lily quickly undid the latch. "Bumble!" she cried as the bee flew into the room. "What are you doing here? What's wrong?"

Bumble buzzed urgently around her

head. Then Lily heard a faint cry come through the open window.

"HEEEEEELP!"

Someone was in trouble! Without changing out of her nightclothes, Lily raced out of the Home Tree. Bumble followed on her heels.

Outside, she met up with Tinker Bell and Rani. They, too, had heard the cry.

"HEEEEEEELP!"

"It's coming from over there," said Tinker Bell. Tink's hair, which normally she wore in a ponytail, was loose around her shoulders. Both Tink and Rani were still wearing their pyjamas. Like Lily, they had come straight from their beds.

Bumble shot off in the direction Tink had pointed. The fairies followed him. The cries were coming from Lily's garden.

When they got there, they saw Pell and Pluck, two harvest-talent fairies. They were dangling from the branches of the mysterious plant.

Pell and Pluck saw them, too. "Help us!" they cried.

Tink flew over and grabbed Pell's hands. She tried to pull her away from the tree. But Pell's wings seemed to be glued to the branch.

Tink looked closer. "They're stuck in sap!" she cried. "We'll need hot water to unstick them!"

Lily grabbed a watering can and ran over to the little stream. She filled it with water, then brought it to Rani. Rani sprinkled a pinch of fairy dust on the water and waved her hand over it. It began to steam.

Holding the watering can between

them, Lily and Tink flew to Pell. Carefully, they poured the hot water over Pell's wings. Slowly, the sap began to loosen. Tink grabbed Pell's wrists.

*Snap!* Pell's wings came free and she dropped. Only Tink's grip on her wrists kept her from falling. Carefully, Tink lowered her to the ground.

Then Tink and Lily flew to Pluck and freed her wings, too.

When both harvest-talent fairies were on the ground, Lily and Rani used more hot water to wash the rest of the sap from their wings. The sap was hard to scrub away, but luckily neither of the fairies' wings had been hurt.

As Lily and Rani worked, Pell and Pluck talked over one another, explaining what had happened. "We woke up early – "

Pell began.

"Like we always do – " Pluck added.

"And came down to the garden to pick raspberries – "

"For breakfast, you know. The cooking fairies were going to make raspberry jam."

"We were flying through the garden – "

"It was still dark out – "

"So we couldn't see anything. And I accidentally bumped against that plant."

"She got stuck!"

"I got stuck! And when Pluck tried to help me, she got stuck, too!"

"And then we heard an owl!"

"We couldn't move."

"We thought he'd catch us for sure!"

"We called and called. We were afraid no one would ever hear us."

"It was so scary."

Pell and Pluck stretched out their wet wings to dry. By now the sun was up. Still, they were shivering in the cool morning air.

"Rani," said Lily, "will you go back to the Home Tree and get some hot tea and – "

" – blankets?" Rani nodded. She put her fingers to her lips and whistled for Brother Dove, who acted as Rani's wings. When he came, Rani climbed on his back and they flew off.

Tink looked at Lily. "The other fairies are going to be upset," she said.

Lily nodded. "I know."

Tink gave Lily's hand a squeeze.

Lily's heart sank. She knew Tink meant to be comforting. But Lily knew what that little squeeze meant.

The worst was still to come.

# 8

Rani returned with several other fairies. Some carried blankets and a clay thermos full of hot tea. Others had come along simply to see what the fuss was about. Ree, the fairy queen, was with them.

"What has happened?" Queen Ree asked.

The two harvest-talent fairies repeated their story.

When they were done, Vidia pushed her way to the front of the crowd. "That vile plant has caused nothing but trouble in Pixie Hollow. It should be cut down!" she cried.

Some fairies in the crowd began to murmur, "She's right. The plant is bad. We should get rid of it."

Lily stood with her hand on the plant's stem. Her heart pounded in her chest. Would they try to uproot the plant right then and there?

Suddenly, Tinker Bell moved over to stand beside the plant, too. She folded her arms across her chest and glared at Vidia and the grumbling fairies.

Lily gave her a grateful look. She knew Tink didn't care much for the plant. But Tink was a good friend. And a brave one.

Just then, a familiar face moved through the crowd. It was Iris. She came to stand next to Lily, Tink, and the plant.

"This is Lily's garden. The plant belongs to her. You can't just chop it down," Iris declared.

"That's right," said another voice. It was Rosetta. She joined Lily, Iris, and

Tink. "This plant has my protection," she declared.

"And mine!"

"And mine!"

More garden fairies came out of the crowd. They gathered around Lily and the plant. Now there were two big groups of fairies facing each other. And everyone looked angry.

"That plant is a menace to all fairies!" Vidia shouted. "Pell and Pluck could have been caught by an owl this morning."

More fairies raised their voices in agreement.

"It's not the plant's fault they were flying in the dark without a lamp!" a garden sparrow man argued.

"That plant is ugly!" cried a light-talent fairy.

"It's a monster!" added a cooking-talent sparrow man.

"*You're* a monster. Plant hater!" a garden-talent fairy snapped back.

"Petalhead!" the sparrow man retorted.

Suddenly, another voice rang out like a bell.

"*Fairies!*"

Everyone turned to look. Queen Ree was standing with her hands on her hips. She glowered at the crowd of fairies before her.

"What a disgrace. This is *not* how we settle a disagreement in Pixie Hollow," said the queen. Her voice sounded cool, but her gaze was stern. Behind her, the queen's four attendants glared at the crowd. "Shouting. Name-calling. I'm disappointed in all of you," the queen declared.

Several fairies in the crowd hung their heads. Vidia lifted her chin defiantly.

"At noon tomorrow we will have a meeting in the courtyard of the Home Tree," said the queen. "All fairies are to attend – that includes you, Vidia."

She fixed the fast-flying fairy with a steely look. Vidia was known for disobeying the queen's commands. Vidia tossed her hair as if she didn't care. But the look on her face said she understood.

"Everyone will have a chance to speak," the queen continued. "Until then, I want all fairies to return to their fairy domains. Now."

Grumbling, the groups of fairies broke up and left.

Lily flew over to Pell and Pluck. "Let me help you carry some raspberries back to the kitchen," she said.

"I think you've done enough," Pell snapped.

"First the wasps, now this," Pluck added.

"From now on, we'll get our raspberries somewhere else," said Pell.

Lifting their chins, the two fairies turned their backs on Lily and flew away.

Lily's heart sank. No one would enjoy her garden as long as the plant was standing. But after taking care of it so lovingly, how could she bear to cut it down?

For the rest of the day, no one was happy. Despite the queen's commands, the fairies couldn't seem to get along.

When a weaving-talent fairy tried to

collect sweetgrass to weave her baskets, the garden fairies snubbed her. The cooking-talent fairies argued with the harvest-talent fairies, and as a result, no one got any lunch. Hungry and cross, a light fairy snapped at a water fairy. The water fairy splashed her, and soon the light fairies and the water fairies weren't speaking to each other. Each talent group was annoyed with the other.

Lily stayed away from the Home Tree. She spent the whole day sitting in the skimpy shade of the mysterious plant. And after a lot of thinking, she came to a decision.

"If the fairies of Pixie Hollow decide that the plant should be cut down, I must not stand in their way," Lily told herself. It pained her to say it. But she knew that the most important thing was keeping the peace in the fairy kingdom.

"I only hope they don't make me do it," she added. Lily had never swung an axe in her life. She didn't think she would be able to.

Just then, Spring, a message-talent fairy, flew quickly into the garden. She landed next to Lily.

Spring seemed to be out of breath. She took a couple of deep gulps of air. "I have a message from the queen," she managed at last.

Lily nodded and waited.

"The meeting has been changed. All fairies are to meet in the courtyard at sundown," Spring explained.

Lily's eyes widened. But it wasn't only because of the message. Something strange was happening behind Spring's head.

A yellow fruit the size of a gooseberry was growing from one of the plant's branches. And it seemed to be getting bigger before Lily's eyes!

"There has been too much fighting," Spring went on. She hadn't noticed Lily's startled expression. "The queen doesn't want to wait until tomorrow to settle this."

But Lily wasn't listening. She gaped at the fruit. It had already grown to the size of a small grape.

*I can't let Spring see this*, Lily thought. *She'll tell the queen, and then the plant will be cut down for sure!*

Quickly, Lily jumped up. She whisked her daisy-petal sun hat off her head and hung it over the rapidly growing fruit.

Spring turned to face her.

Lily smiled innocently. "Courtyard at sundown," she repeated. "I'll be there." She was eager to get Spring out of her garden as quickly as possible.

Spring nodded. "Good. Well, I'm off. I've got to get the message to the rest of the fairy kingdom. If you see anyone, you'll be sure to let them know?"

"Yes – oh!" Lily gasped. Out of the corner of her eye, she saw another odd fruit growing from a branch nearby.

"What is it?" Spring started to turn.

Lily sprang into the air, blocking Spring's view. She hovered there, dramatically clutching her foot. *Think fast*, Lily told herself. "I mean – ow! I just stepped on a pine needle!" she exclaimed.

Spring looked at the ground. There was no pine needle in sight. In fact, there wasn't a pine tree anywhere near Lily's garden. She gave Lily a curious look.

"Well, then, see you tonight," Spring

said.

Lily nodded. "Fly safely," she sang cheerily.

When Spring was gone, Lily breathed a sigh of relief. Then she stepped back to look at the plant. Yellow fruits with bumpy skin were growing from all its branches. They got bigger and bigger before Lily's eyes. And, Lily noticed with dismay, uglier and uglier.

Lily clutched her head unhappily. If anyone saw the plant now... She couldn't finish the thought.

She glanced at the sun. It was low in the sky – almost time for the sunset meeting. *If I can keep anyone from seeing the plant before then*, Lily thought, *there might still be a chance to save it.*

# 9

THE SUN WAS sinking on the horizon as the fairies made their way to the roots of the Home Tree. Already the courtyard was in shadow. Light fairies posted themselves all around its edges, brightening the space with their glow.

When all the fairies were present, Queen Ree took her place before the crowd.

"Fairies of Never Land," she declared in her clear and noble voice, "there has never been such a disgraceful day in the fairy kingdom."

"It's that plant!" someone called out.

"The plant! The plant is the cause of the trouble!" more fairies chimed in.

The queen held up a hand to quiet them. "Is the plant the trouble?" she asked evenly. "Or is it the fairies? I wonder. Can you blame a single plant for the unkindness fairies have shown each other this afternoon? If you can prove that to me, we will remove the plant."

The fairies began to murmur. Again, the queen silenced them with her hand. "Every fairy will have a chance to speak. Who will go first?"

"The plant belongs to Lily!" Tinker Bell called out.

Other fairies echoed her. "Yes, it's Lily's. Let her speak first!"

Lily found herself being pushed to the front of the crowd. She had never felt so many fairy eyes on her before, and her heart raced. She took a deep breath.

"Yes, it's true," she said. "I planted the seed in my garden, and I took care of it."

"What kind of plant is it?" Queen Ree asked.

Lily shook her head. "I don't know. I found the seed in the forest. I'd never seen one before. But I think it's a good plant – "

Again, some fairies began to grumble.

"She doesn't even know what it is!"

"Good? It isn't good for anything!"

The queen waited until the crowd quieted down. Then she asked, "Lily, do you think the plant is the cause of all the trouble in Pixie Hollow?"

Before Lily could answer, a voice suddenly shouted, "Wait!"

Everyone turned to look as a breathless Iris flew into the courtyard. She was carrying a yellow object the size and shape of a lemon.

"Wait! Wait!" Iris cried again. She

landed on the ground in front of the crowd of fairies. "Everyone, look! The plant grew fruit."

All the other fairies crowded around to see the strange fruit.

Only Lily stayed where she was. She buried her face in her hands. The secret was out. Now there was no chance of saving the plant.

"What is it?" the fairies murmured. Lily sneaked a look at the fruit. The bumpy, ugly skin was gone. Now it had a pearly sheen that almost seemed to glow. Curious, some fairies reached out to touch it.

"Careful!" someone cried. "It might be poisonous!"

At once, the crowd drew back.

"It's not poisonous," Iris said. "And what's more, I know what it is."

Everyone, including Lily, looked at her in surprise.

"Well," said the queen, "what is it?"

Iris smiled mysteriously. "Come with me," she said.

With Iris leading the way, all the fairies of Pixie Hollow set out for Lily's garden. Soon they saw the strange plant.

Several fairies gasped in surprise. The plant's branches were heavy with clusters of round, golden fruit.

Iris turned to one of the light-talent fairies. "Fira," she said, "will you and your fairies give us some light?"

Fira and the other light-talent fairies brightened their glows. They surrounded the plant, covering it with their light.

"Ah!" the crowd of fairies sighed. The golden fruit glowed in the light. The plant looked very beautiful.

"Now watch," said Iris. She flew up and grasped one of the fruits. Using all her might, she gave it a tug. The fruit came away in her arms.

Immediately, another fruit grew in place of the one she had just plucked.

Lily's hand flew to her mouth. The fairies around her gasped. Even the queen looked stunned.

"What is it?" she asked again.

"I'll show you," Iris replied. She set the fruit on the ground and opened her book. She held up a page. On it was a drawing of a tree. Its drooping branches were full of round, glowing fruit. The drawing was labeled "Ever Tree" in Iris's handwriting.

"It flowers only once, then grows fruit forever and ever. That's why it's called an

Ever tree," Iris explained.

"Can you eat the fruit?" the queen asked.

Iris asked Tink for her dagger. She split open the skin of the fruit she'd picked.

Inside were golden pips, not unlike the red ones of a pomegranate. Iris plucked a pip out and popped it in her mouth. "Yes," she said as honey-coloured juice dribbled down her chin. "It's delicious."

Several fairies reached for the pips. Iris handed one to Lily. When she bit into it, it tasted like ice-cold lemonade on a hot day. Satisfying and perfect.

"But how did you know what it was?" Lily asked Iris.

"I heard about the Ever tree a long time ago," Iris explained. "So long ago that I'd almost forgotten about it. Of course, I drew the picture as it was described to me and wrote down everything I heard.

"Many, many years ago, before there were any fairies here, Ever trees grew all over Never Land. Then the volcano on Torth Mountain erupted and all the trees burned. Every last one.

"There was only one Ever seed known to be left," Iris went on. "But the dragon Kyto selfishly hoarded it in his collection of rare treasures."

At the mention of Kyto, several fairies shuddered and looked toward Torth Mountain, home of the dragon's prison lair. Kyto was wicked through and through.

"But how did the seed get here?" Tinker Bell asked.

Iris shrugged. "I guess it blew out of his lair. If Lily hadn't found it and planted it so carefully, Never Land might never have seen another Ever tree. Ever trees are very fragile, you know. They need lots of care."

Everyone turned to look at Lily.

She ducked her head shyly. "Iris helped," she said simply.

Several more fairies had clustered around the fruit and were gobbling its pips.

"I could make a delicious tart out of this juice," said Dulcie.

"This fruit would make excellent jam," said Pell. Pluck nodded.

Even Vidia was eating the Ever fruit, though she quickly hid it behind her back when Lily looked her way. But a moment later, she shrugged and pulled it out again. "It's good," she said grudgingly, and went back to eating.

More fairies began to pull fruit from

the plant's branches. Suddenly, Queen Ree cried, "Stop!"

The fairies froze. They looked at the queen, startled.

"This plant belongs to Lily," said the queen. "It's up to her whether she wants to share it."

All the fairies turned to Lily.

Lily looked around at them and grinned. "Of course I want to share," she said. "Everyone is welcome."

The fairies cheered. And they spent the rest of the night eating Ever fruit and dancing beneath the plant's branches.

# 10

LILY LAY ON a soft patch of moss in the corner of her garden. All day long her garden had bustled with activity as fairies dropped by to pick fruit from the Ever tree. The cooking-talent fairies needed several of the fruits to make a special dessert. The healing-talent fairies wanted to see if the fruit could be used to treat illnesses. And hungry fairies from all the talents came by to get a snack.

Lily loved having all the visitors. But now she was tired. She wanted nothing more than to relax on the moss and watch the grass grow.

She had just spotted a blade of grass that needed her attention when a shrill voice interrupted her thoughts.

"Goodness, what a day!"

Lily closed her eyes and sighed. Then she sat up and said, "Hello, Iris."

Iris plopped down beside Lily on the moss. "What a day I've had!" she declared. "I've been around to five different gardens today. All the garden fairies want me to write about their gardens. I've had to add more pages to my book."

She held up her book, which was fatter than ever.

"And the other fairies! Every little seed they find, they bring to me. They think it's another Ever tree. Of course, they're all just ordinary flower seeds.

"But don't worry, Lily," Iris went on, "I made sure to save time for you. Now, tell me about your marigolds."

She opened to a blank leaf in her book

and set her writing splinter on the page.

Lily frowned, confused. "What about them?" she asked.

"Why, they're so golden! They should be called *more*-igolds, don't you think?"

Iris laughed at her own joke.

And this time, Lily laughed along with her.

Join Tinker Bell, Prilla and all
the other Never Fairies in
the next Disney Fairies book...

# The Trouble
# with Tink

Here is a fairy-sized preview
of the first chapter!

The
Trouble
with
Tink

# 1

ONE SUNNY, BREEZY afternoon in Pixie Hollow, Tinker Bell sat in her workshop, frowning at a copper pot. With one hand, she clutched her tinker's hammer, and with the other, she tugged at her blond fringe, which was Tink's habit when she was thinking hard about something. The pot had been squashed nearly flat on one side. Tink was trying to determine how to tap it to make it right again.

All around Tink lay her tinkering tools: baskets full of rivets, scraps of tin, pliers, iron wire, and swatches of steel wool for scouring a pot until it shone. On the walls hung portraits of some of the pans and ladles and washtubs Tink had mended. Tough jobs were always Tink's favourites.

Tink was a pots-and-pans fairy, and her greatest joy came from fixing things. She loved anything metal that could be cracked or dented. Even her workshop was made from a teakettle that had once belonged to a Clumsy.

*Ping! Ping! Ping!* Tink began to pound away. Beneath Tink's hammer the copper moved as easily as if she were smoothing the folds in a blanket.

Tink had almost finished when a shadow fell across her worktable. She looked up and saw a dark figure silhouetted in the sunny doorway. The edges of the silhouette sparkled.

"Oh, hi, Terence. Come in," said Tink.

Terence moved out of the sunlight and into the room, but he continued to shimmer. Terence was a dust-talent sparrow man. He measured and handed out the fairy dust that allowed Never Land's fairies to fly and do their magic. As a result, he was dustier than most fairies, and he sparkled all the time.

"Hi, Tink. Are you working? I mean, I see you're working. Are you almost done? That's a nice pot," Terence said, all in a rush.

"It's Violet's pot. They're dyeing spider silk tomorrow, and she needs it for boiling the dye," Tink replied. She looked eagerly at Terence's hands and sighed when she saw that they were empty. Terence stopped by Tink's workshop nearly every day. Often he brought a broken pan or a mangled sieve for her to fix. Other times, like now, he just brought himself.

"That's right, tomorrow is dyeing day," said Terence. "I saw the harvest talents bringing in the blueberries for the dye earlier. They've got a good crop this year, they should get a nice deep blue colour..."

As Terence rambled on, Tink looked longingly at the copper pot. She picked up her hammer, then reluctantly put it back down. *It would be rude to start tapping right now,* she thought. Tink liked talking to Terence. But she liked tinkering more.

"Anyway, Tink, I just wanted to let you know that they're starting a game of tag in the meadow. I thought maybe you'd like to join in," Terence finished.

Tink's wing tips quivered. It had been ages since there had been a game of fairy tag. Suddenly, she felt herself bursting with the desire to play, the way you fill up with a sneeze just before it explodes.

She glanced down at the pot again.

The dent was nearly smooth. Tink thought she could easily play a game of tag and still have time to finish her work before dinner.

Standing up, she slipped her tinker's hammer into a loop on her belt and smiled at Terence.

"Let's go," she said.

When Tink and Terence got to the meadow, the game of tag was already in full swing. Everywhere spots of bright colour wove in and out of the tall grass as fairies darted after each other.

Fairy tag is different from the sort of tag that humans, or Clumsies, as the fairies call them, play. For one thing, the fairies fly rather than run. For another, the fairies don't just chase each other until one is tagged "it." If that were the case, the fast-flying-talent fairies would win every time.

In fairy tag, the fairies and sparrow men all use their talents to try to win. And when a fairy is tagged, by being tapped on her head and told "Choose you," that fairy's whole talent group – or at least all those who are playing – becomes "chosen." Games of fairy tag are large, complicated, and very exciting.

As Tink and Terence joined the game, a huge drop of water came hurtling through the air at them. Terence ducked, and the drop splashed against a dandelion behind him. The water-talent fairies were "chosen," Tink realised.

As they sped through the tall grass, the water fairies hurled balls of water at the other fairies. When the balls hit, they burst like water balloons and dampened the fairies' wings. This slowed them down, which helped the water fairies gain on them.

Already the other talents had organised their defence. The animal-talent fairies, led by Beck and Fawn, had rounded up a crew of chipmunks to ride when their wings got too wet to fly. The light-talent fairies bent the sunshine as they flew through it, so rays of light always shone in the eyes of the fairies chasing them. Tink saw that the pots-and-pans fairies had used washtubs to create makeshift catapults. They were trying to catch the balls of water and fling them back at the water fairies.

As Tink zipped down to join them, she heard a voice above her call, "Watch out, Tinker Bell! I'll choose you!" She looked up. Her friend Rani, a water-talent fairy, was circling above her on the back of a dove. Rani was the only fairy in the kingdom who didn't have wings. She'd cut hers off to help save Never Land when Mother Dove's egg had been destroyed. Now Brother Dove did her flying for her.

Rani lifted her arm and hurled a water ball. It wobbled through the air and splashed harmlessly on the ground, inches away from Tink. Tink laughed, and so did Rani.

"I'm such a terrible shot!" Rani cried happily.

Just then, the pots-and-pans fairies fired a catapult. The water flew at Rani and drenched her. Rani laughed even harder.

*"Choose you!"*

The shout rang through the meadow. All the fairies stopped midflight and turned. A water-talent fairy named Tally was standing over Jerome, a dust-talent sparrow man. Her hand was on his head.

"Dust talent!" Jerome sang out.

Abruptly, the fairies rearranged themselves. Anyone who happened to be near a dust-talent fairy immediately darted away. The other fairies hovered in the air, waiting to see what the dust talents would do.

Tink caught sight of Terence near a tree stump a few feet away. Terence grinned at her. She coyly smiled back – and then she bolted. In a flash, Terence was after her.

Tink dove into an azalea bush. Terence was right on her heels. Tink's sides ached with laughter, but she kept flying. She wove in and out of the bush's branches. She made a hairpin turn around a thick branch. Then she dashed toward an opening in the leaves and headed back to the open meadow.

But suddenly, the twigs in front of her closed like a gate. Tink skidded to a stop and watched as the twigs wrapped around themselves. With a flick of fairy dust, Terence had closed the branches of the bush. It was the simplest magic. But Tink was trapped.

She turned as Terence flew up to her.

"Choose you," he said, placing his hand on her head. But he said it softly. None of the rest of the fairies could have heard.

Just then, a shout rang out across the meadow: "Hawk!"

At once, Tink and Terence dropped down under the azalea bush's branches. Through the leaves, Tink could see the other fairies ducking for cover. The scout who had spotted the hawk hid in the branches of a nearby elm tree. The entire meadow seemed to hold its breath as the hawk's shadow moved across it.

When it was gone, the fairies waited a few moments, then slowly came out of their hiding places. But the mood had changed. The game of tag was over.

Tink and Terence climbed out of the bush.

"I must finish Violet's pot before dinner," Tink told Terence. "Thank you for telling me about the game."

"I'm really glad you came, Tink," said Terence. He gave her a sparkling smile, but Tink didn't see it. She was already flying away, thinking about the copper pot.

Tink's fingers itched to begin working

again. As she neared her workshop, she reached for her tinker's hammer hanging on her belt. Her fingertips touched the leather loop.

Tink stopped flying. Frantically, she ran her fingers over the belt loop again and again. Her hammer was gone.

# Collect all the Disney Fairies books

## Discover the story of the Never Fairies in
## Fairy Dust and the Quest for the Egg

## Coming soon!